JinJin AND RAIN WIZARD

For Chadd and Stuart, Pam and Kurt.
G. C.

AUTHOR'S NOTE

As a little girl growing up in China, I ate rice at every meal. Like all Chinese children I learned to use chopsticks skillfully, picking up every grain of rice until my bowl was empty and clean. My grandmother often cooked rice with a variety of ingredients. I could eat a mountain of rice when she made my favorite dish — rice with pineapples and cashew nuts!

What bread is to people in the West, rice is to people in the East. It is vital to daily life—more precious than pearls or jade. My childhood memories of rice, along with its long history as a significant part of Chinese culture, inspired me to write *Jin Jin and Rain Wizard*, my second book about this magical little dragon.

ACKNOWLEDGMENTS

This book was made possible through the help of many loving and inspiring people. My special thanks go to my amazing editor, Claudia Bedrick. I would also like to give thanks to my agent, Tina Wexler, and my mentor, Lewis Frumkes, as well as to Abigail Bedrick, Anne Anderson, Adam Carlson, Paul Colin, Adam Doyle, Millicent Fairhurst, Bernette Ford and Judi Miller.

Published by Enchanted Lion Books,
201 Richards Street, Studio 4,
Brooklyn, NY 11231
Text and Illustrations © 2009 by Grace Chang.
All rights reserved under International and
Pan-American Copyright Conventions.
[A CIP record is on file with the Library of Congress]
ISBN: 978-1-59270-086-8
Production Director: Millicent Fairhurst
The artwork in this book was created with Chinese watercolor
Typeset in Dante
Printed in China by South China Printing Company, Ltd.

JinJin AND RAIN WIZARD

GRACE CHANG   Illustrated by **CHONG CHANG**

ENCHANTED LION BOOKS
NEW YORK

練 Exercise

One summer morning as the sun climbed over the mountains and the birds twittered in the trees, Jin Jin sprang from his bed and hopped out the window.

"Next time please use the door," Old Turtle called from his rocker.

"And come back for breakfast when you're done," sang Crane from the kitchen.

Jin Jin joined the early risers who had gathered for Tai Chi.

"Let's begin!" Jin Jin called out happily. As he said, "Reach for the sky," Jin Jin and his friends gently stroked the air. When he said, "Breathe in," they all pulled back their arms as if reining in horses.

"And now..." Jin Jin opened his mouth wide, preparing to spray out water. Getting cooled off by Jin Jin's dragon shower was everyone's favorite part of the morning workout.

Making a big O with his lips Jin Jin blew hard, but no water came out — only a blast of dry air. "Maybe I haven't warmed up enough," he said to himself, giving his shoulders a shake. He blew again with all his might, but it was no use.

"I don't understand," Jin Jin mumbled.

"Maybe it's the weather," said Tutu the hare. "Look, there isn't a cloud in the sky."

"But the clouds have nothing to do with me."

Jin Jin turned away, dragging his tail behind him.

迷 A Puzzle

Jin Jin stared blankly at his rice rolls. "How come I can't breathe out water anymore?"

Old Turtle handed him some chopsticks. "Let's see if we can figure it out."

"Maybe you're hungry," said Crane, sliding the plate closer.

"No thanks," said Jin Jin. "I'm still full from yesterday's rice festival."

Jin Jin rubbed his stomach, recalling how he had filled his bowl again and again. Rice dishes swam before his eyes: rice porridge, pudding, dumplings, pancakes, noodles, bread, Dim Sum, crackers, and even rice candies.

Old Turtle peered over his spectacles. "There certainly was a lot of food."

"I really stuffed myself!" exclaimed Jin Jin. "I couldn't even finish my fifth bowl."

"What did you do with the leftovers?" Old Turtle asked kindly.

"I threw them away."

Crane's beak flew open. "You should never ever do that, Jin Jin. Rice is as precious as gold."

"It was just a handful," said Jin Jin. "How can so little matter?"

"Let's get some fresh air and see what we can find out," said Old Turtle. Soon the three found themselves in a place that Jin Jin had never seen before.

A pagoda-style archway towered over them. Its curved roof gleamed like gold.

"Where are we?" asked Jin Jin.

"This is the way to Ancient Times," said Old Turtle, his eyes twinkling. "By passing through this archway you just might discover why you can no longer breathe out water."

Crane handed Jin Jin a gourd. "This is for you to take with you."

"What's in it?" asked Jin Jin, trying to open it.

"Wait," said Old Turtle. "Save it for someone in great need."

Jin Jin shook the gourd and heard it rattle. Then, taking a deep breath, he bowed goodbye and stepped through the archway.

古村 An Ancient Village

As Jin Jin traveled farther and farther from home, he nibbled on Goji berries and enjoyed the warm breeze rippling over his golden scales. Gradually the landscape changed from green to yellow to orange to red and finally to brown, as if the seasons had slipped by. In the distance he saw a small village.

There Jin Jin met a gaunt villager who offered him a bit of bamboo shoot. "It's not much," he said wearily, "but as you can see, we are in great need."

"In great need …" thought Jin Jin, remembering Old Turtle's words. Taking the gourd from his shoulder, he said, "I think this might help you."

The man removed the lid and the two peered inside. "It's rice!" shouted Jin Jin.

"Rice?" asked the man. "What's rice?"

Amazed, Jin Jin realized that he had traveled back to a time before rice existed. "All you have to do is plant these in watery soil," he said, "and food will grow."

"But this is so little," said the man, letting the grains fall to the ground. "Besides, we get no rain. Rain Wizard has abandoned us."

"Where did this Rain Wizard go?" asked Jin Jin.

"He lives somewhere in that cloud." The villager pointed. "We think he's sleeping. We've tried to wake him by playing flutes, banging on pots and shouting until we lost our voices, but nothing has worked."

"I think I might be able to wake him up!" Jin Jin cried. With an enormous leap he soared into the sky, flying higher and higher until he could no longer be seen from the ground.

解 A Solution

Jin Jin had never flown so high. Spreading his arms he sailed over a cottony forest. From somewhere nearby he heard a deep rumbling. Startled, Jin Jin lost his balance and sank into a gigantic cloud. Through the mist he saw something that took his breath away. It was a magnificent palace.

"RAIN WIZARD," read the sign above the entrance.
"This must be the place," Jin Jin whispered, and without warning, the immense doors creaked open.

The rumbling grew louder. Fighting against a fierce wind, Jin Jin inched his way inside. "If I weren't a dragon, I might be afraid," he thought.

To his surprise, the tremendous noise was the incredibly loud snoring of an old man. His white beard and eyebrows were so long that Jin Jin couldn't tell where they began or ended. Only when he tripped over some lightning bolts was he sure that the old man was Rain Wizard!

To gently rouse the wizard, Jin Jin sang, "Lai, Lai. Chi-lai. Come, come. Get up."

The old man did not stir. "Get UP!" Jin Jin sang more boldly. Still nothing.

"This is not working," Jin Jin thought. Climbing onto the bed, Jin Jin tugged at the long beard and shouted, "Wake up, wake UP, WAAAKE UP!"

The old man's eyes popped open. "I hear you. No need to shout," he yawned. "Why are you interrupting my nap?"

"I'm sorry, Honorable One," Jin Jin replied. "The villagers below need water."

"Why don't you give it to them? You're a dragon!"

"Well, I've . . . I've lost my water-breathing powers."

"What? That's nonsense! Let me see. Say 'Aaaaaahhh'."

"Ah," said Jin Jin.

"Louder. Sing out!"

"Aaahhh, aaaahhh."

"Mm-hmm, I see the problem. A piece of rice is stuck in your water-breathing pipe."

"Maybe I ate too much at the rice festival?" Jin Jin asked hopefully.

"That's not the problem. It's good to enjoy yourself. Tell me more."

"Well…I also threw some rice away."

"I see. So you wasted it."

Jin Jin lowered his head. "Now I'll never breathe out water again."

"But it's never too late to correct a mistake," encouraged Rain Wizard. He reached for a large fistful of lightning bolts and tossed one to Jin Jin. "Follow me!"

They stepped onto a nearby cloud. Rain Wizard hurled several bolts earthward. The sound of thunder filled the sky.

"Ready, aim, fire!" cried Jin Jin happily as he threw down his bolt.

Jin Jin's whole body shook as thunder boomed all around him.

With a pop, the piece of rice flew out of Jin Jin's mouth. He felt moisture rising from his lungs.

"What's happening?" he asked as little clouds floated from his mouth. Jin Jin watched his clouds rise higher and higher. As they expanded and melted together, torrents of rain poured down.

Below the villagers danced with joy, pressing the seeds that Jin Jin had brought deeper and deeper into the wet soil. Soon green shoots began to appear.

"They've just made their first rice paddy!" Jin Jin cried out, "And I've made my first rain clouds!"

"Look," said Rain Wizard. "Some clouds are floating away."

"Where are they going?" asked Jin Jin.

"To your home, I think."

"Not without me!"

"Then you must take the short cut," said Rain Wizard, unfurling his long beard. Jin Jin hopped on, bowed goodbye and slid all the way down to the ground.

Once down Jin Jin scampered past the Goji bushes, through the ancient archway, and home to his hut.

Old Turtle sat in his rocker and Crane stood by her earthen stove, heating up rice rolls. "Ni-Hao!" they called, greeting Jin Jin with open arms.

Tutu the hare appeared at the corner of the hut. "Can we finish Tai Chi now?"

"Yes!" cried Jin Jin merrily, and they dashed up the hill to find their friends.

Jin Jin felt good to be home. "Here we go! Let's begin!"

While pulling back his arms he heard gurgling inside him. "That's coming from me," he said.

His friends leaned in closer.

"All right, back to your positions."

Jin Jin paused for a moment, sniffing the delicious aroma of the rice rolls. He thought about dipping them into tangy sauce and savoring their crunchiness.

This time he knew he would lick his rice bowl clean, polishing it to reflect his happy dragon face.

The Story of Rice

No matter how you like your rice—steamed or fried, with broccoli or pineapple, or even curry—there are more ways to eat it than you can imagine. Do you know that rice has fed more people over a longer period of time than any other grain?

Six thousand years have passed since rice first appeared in China. Myth holds that a disastrous flood occurred that destroyed all plant life, leaving people with nothing to eat. One day a mysterious dog came to a village, bearing yellow seeds that accidentally fell onto some watery soil. No one paid any attention until some green sprouts burst out of the muddy ground. With that, we are told, the first rice paddy appeared.

Rice grows only in warm climates, in fields flooded with water. Paddies are often divided into squares. If you were to catch a glimpse of some from an airplane, they would resemble a glistening chessboard.

From ancient China, rice spread to India, Greece, Egypt, the Mediterranean and Europe. It traveled all around the world, and eventually to North America, which is how it found its way onto your plate.

There are many varieties of rice: white rice, red rice, brown rice, sticky rice and on and on. Rice can be ground into flour to make cakes, bread, dumplings and more. It is thought that the very first ice cream came from China. Composed of a mixture of rice, sugar, milk and snow, what was once known as "rice cream" eventually become today's ice cream.

Rice can also be used for other purposes besides food. In ancient times, people folded layers of cloth coated with sticky rice to fashion the soles of their shoes. They also used sticky rice mixed with powdered stone as mortar to join bricks in the construction of houses. Believe it or not, the buildings of the Forbidden City in Beijing, once the home of emperors, and even the Great Wall of China are cemented with sticky rice!

Character for RICE

The Legend of Rain Wizard

According to Chinese legend, Rain Wizard is the one who makes it rain. For this reason, farmers have worshiped him in the belief that by doing so they would gain his favor. As a result, giant wooden statues of Rain Wizard holding an umbrella can often be seen in Chinese temples, while smaller ones are often found in the kitchens of farmers.

Folktales describe Rain Wizard as a wise, happy, but temperamental figure. He can travel from the sky down to Earth quicker than the lightning bolts he hurls to make thunderstorms. When summoned he usually brings normal rain showers; but when he is sad and cries, then the rain comes in bursts, followed by dry spells. First the crops drown in too much water, and then they grow parched from too little. When there is no rain, farmers worry that Rain Wizard has overslept and will wake up hungry and in a bad mood. To make sure that he has enough to eat, people set up a shrine with a clay figurine of Rain Wizard holding an umbrella. Next to it they leave a bowl of rice to be certain that he is well fed.

Ages ago farmers used to ask dragons for water and the wizard in the sky for rain. As time went by the Chinese dragon became a symbol of prosperity, power and good fortune, while Rain Wizard remained associated simply with rain.

The success or failure of the harvest once depended completely on nature. Rainfall could determine whether people prospered or starved. Now farmers can irrigate their crops even if it doesn't rain. All the same, here and there farmers still put out little bowls of rice for Rain Wizard — just in case.

Character for RAIN WIZARD